Stewie Boomstein Starts School

Written by
Christine Bronstein

Illustrated by
Karen Young

To Roan, Grace, Caleb, Charlotte and
our fabulous husbands Phil and Michael

Nothing But The Truth, LLC
980 Magnolia Avenue, Suite C-6
Larkspur, CA 94939

Stewie Boomstein Starts School and Stewie Boomstein Starts School Cover Design are trademarks of Nothing But The Truth, LLC.
For information about book purchases please visit the Nothing But The Truth website at NothingButtheTruth.com
Also available in ebook.
Library of Congress Control Number: 2014940989

Stewie Boomstein Starts School
By Christine Bronstein
Illustrations by Karen Young
ISBN 978-0-9883754-9-9 (paperback)
ISBN 978-0-9904652-0-1 (hardcover)
ISBN 978-0-9904652-1-8 (ePub ebook)

Printed in the United States of America
Design by ALL Publications, Portland, Oregon
First Edition

My name is Stewie Boomstein,
and I like to know what happens next.
I like to know because there are
a lot of things that I do not like.

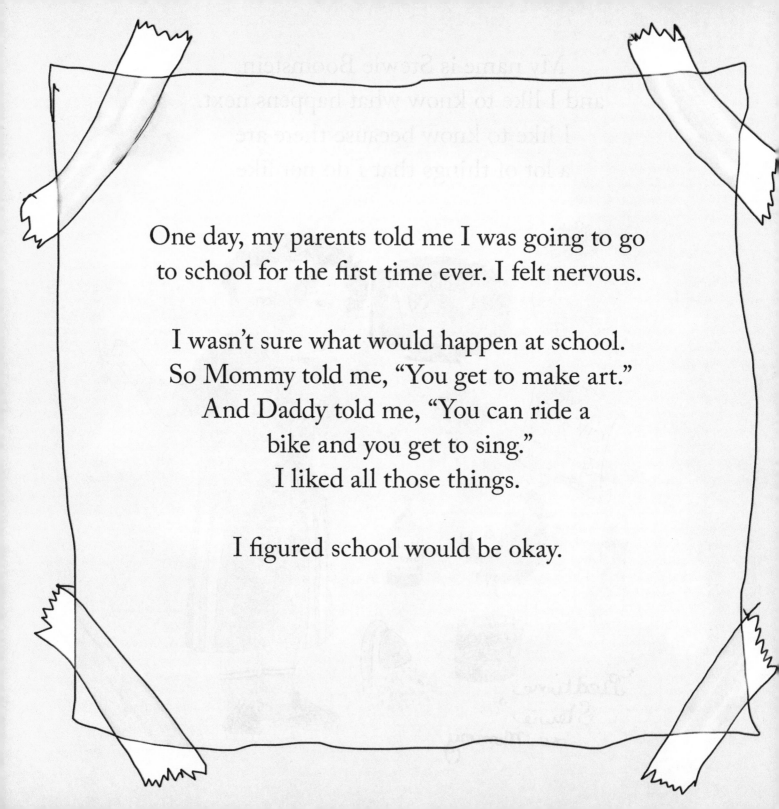

One day, my parents told me I was going to go
to school for the first time ever. I felt nervous.

I wasn't sure what would happen at school.
So Mommy told me, "You get to make art."
And Daddy told me, "You can ride a
bike and you get to sing."
I liked all those things.

I figured school would be okay.

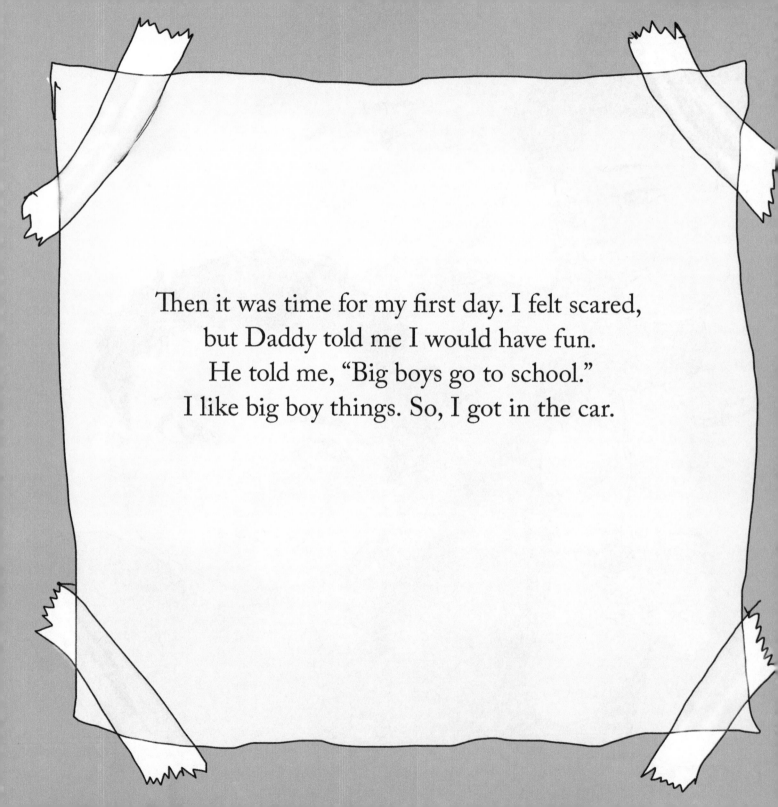

Then it was time for my first day. I felt scared,
but Daddy told me I would have fun.
He told me, "Big boys go to school."
I like big boy things. So, I got in the car.

When we got to school,
Daddy showed me around the classroom
and then the teacher said, "All Daddies and
Mommies have to leave now."

That made me sad and feeling sad
makes me mad.

Then, when I was feeling a little less mad because
I was playing with a cool train, the teacher said,
"It is time for Arts and Crafts."

I like art, but I don't like to be
told when to make art.

Then suddenly, it was time to play outside.
There were bikes, but I wasn't in the mood.

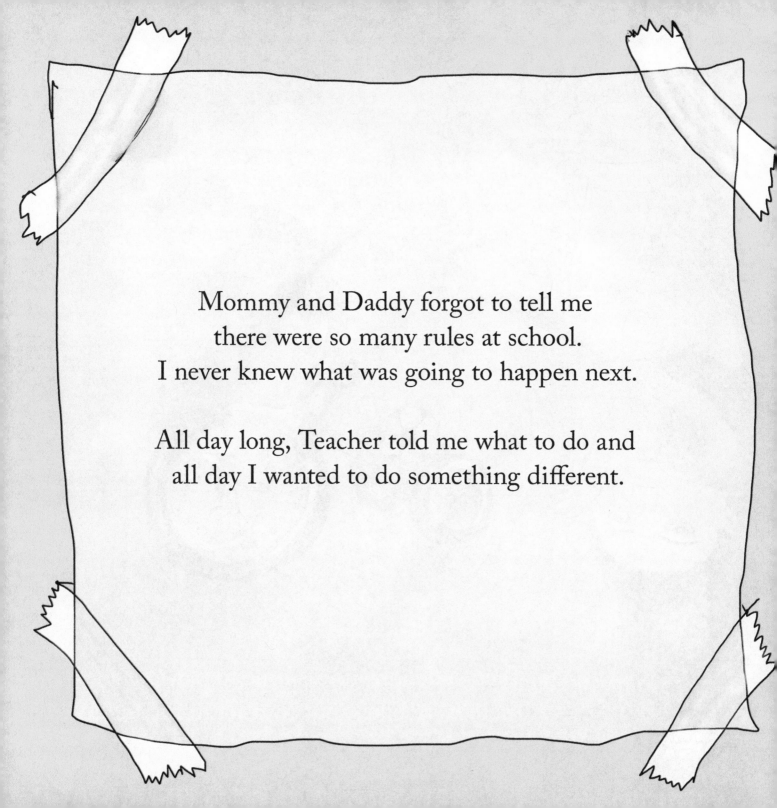

Mommy and Daddy forgot to tell me
there were so many rules at school.
I never knew what was going to happen next.

All day long, Teacher told me what to do and
all day I wanted to do something different.

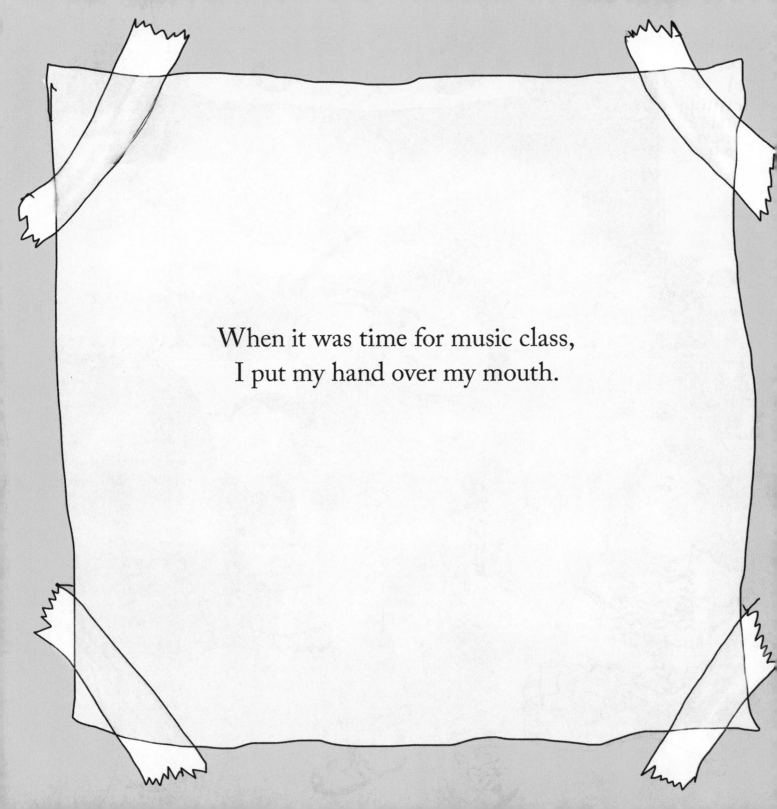

When it was time for music class,
I put my hand over my mouth.

When it was time to nap I asked the teacher,

Can you get me outta here?

She just looked at me.

"NO ONE TOLD ME I HAD TO NAP!"
I boomed.

I wouldn't lie on my mat,
so Teacher called my Mommy.

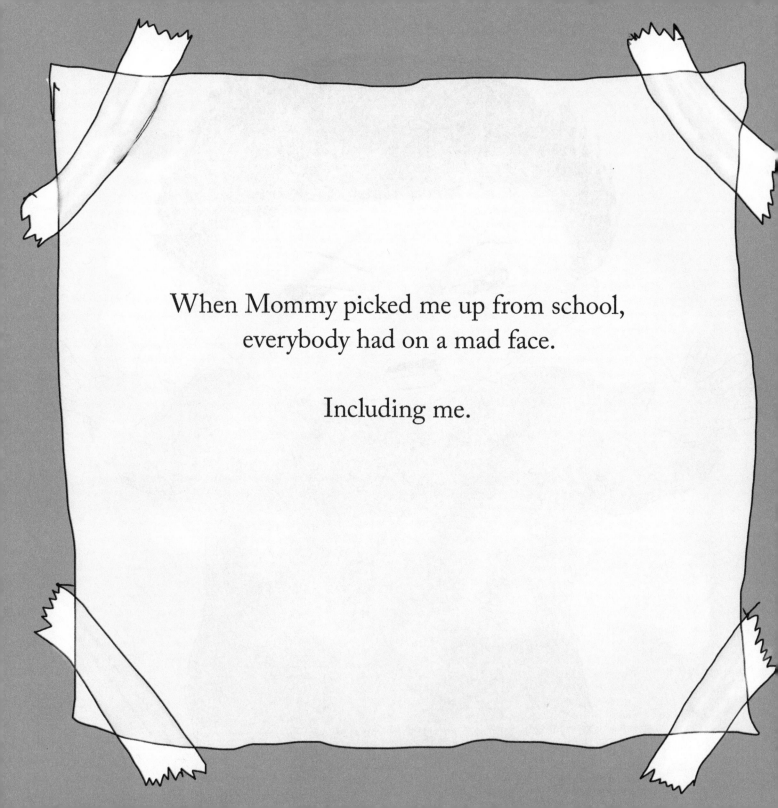

When Mommy picked me up from school,
everybody had on a mad face.

Including me.

At home my big brother, Zoom, asked why
everybody was wearing a mad face.

"I don't like school," I told him from the
time-out chair Mommy made me sit in
when we got home.

"Why? You get to play all day," he said as
he zoomed around the dinner table to
give me a picture he drew.

"I never knew what was going to happen next.
I didn't know when Mommy was coming and
no one told me I had to nap," I told Zoom.
"It was terrible!"

My little sister, Princess Penelope, gave me
a big wiggly hug to make me feel better.

"Tomorrow will be better," Mommy said
when she put me to bed that night.

I tried to fall asleep but my whole body felt mad.
A list kept running through my head of all
the things I was mad about.

There were two things I wasn't mad about:
Zoom drew me a cool picture and
Princess Penelope gave me a hug
to make me feel better.

Then, I looked at my cozy blanket
with all the boxes on it.

"I HAVE AN IDEA!"
I boomed and woke up the whole house.

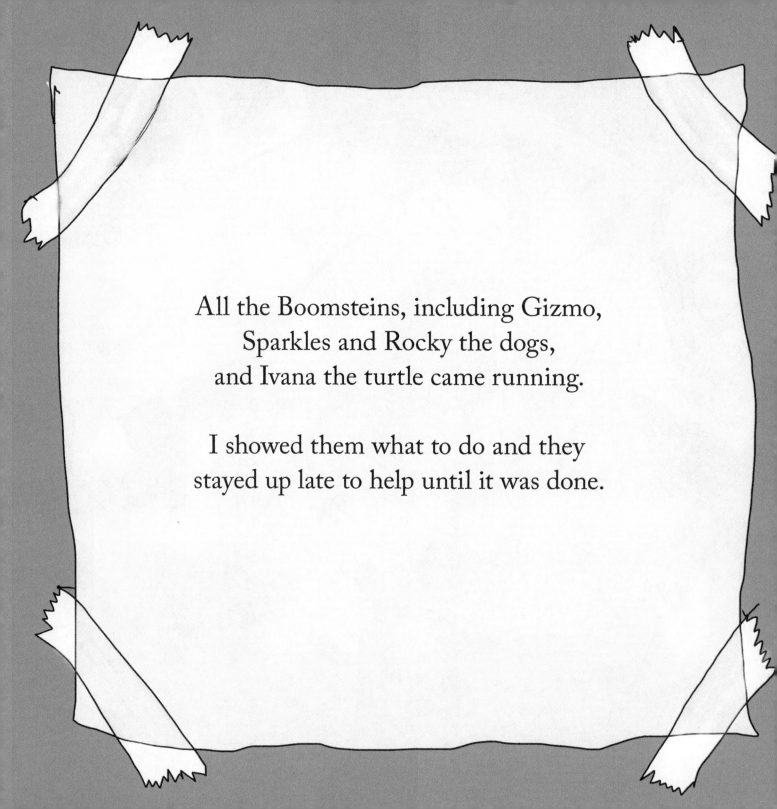

All the Boomsteins, including Gizmo,
Sparkles and Rocky the dogs,
and Ivana the turtle came running.

I showed them what to do and they
stayed up late to help until it was done.

The next day at school,
when it was time to create art,
I drew a picture for Zoom.

When it was time to play outside,
I rode a bike all around the
play yard with a friend.

And when it was music time,
I sang the loudest.
(I am a Boomstein, after all.)

The teacher was curious.
"What's that piece of paper you
keep looking at, Stewie?"she asked me.

"My family made it for me, in the
middle of the night," I told her.
"It's my What Happens Next
picture schedule."

I showed Teacher how the paper had
little drawings of everything that was
going to happen that day at school.

"I like to know what's going to
happen next," I said.

When Mommy picked me up from school
that day, everybody had on a happy face.
Including me.

On the way to the car,
I looked at my paper and asked,

But Mommy,
what happens next?

Stewie's Mom Interviews the Experts
How to Prepare You and Your Child for School

The Experts: Dr. Meryl Lipton MD, PhD and
Dr. Barbara Kalmanson PhD

Stewie's Mom: What can parents do ahead of time to make their child's first day of school easier?

Experts: Giving children as much information as possible about what will happen at school is crucial. For example, parents can start practicing the school morning routine in advance, so the children become used to waking up on their new schedule, and getting dressed and ready to go on time.

Children will benefit from familiarity with the school and their new classmates. Parents can take their children by the school and to play on the playground. If your school provides a contact list of the other families, you can set up play dates for your child with his or her new classmates before school starts.

Stewie's Mom: Aside from a contact list, what other helpful information can schools provide?

Experts: Parents can ask for information about: the routine for parent-child separation, exact time class begins, daily schedule, what concepts and materials will be taught, and what books will be read

Find out if you can bring your child to visit the teacher in his or her classroom before the school year starts.

Stewie's Mom: What if my school doesn't offer any of those things?

Experts: Make an appointment to meet with the teacher in advance. You can share what you learn with your child and answer any questions your child has about what to expect.

Stewie's Mom: You mentioned that I should find out about the concepts and materials the class uses. Can you be more specific about how that will help my child?

Experts: We can't emphasize enough that you want to set expectations and create familiarity so your child feels comfortable. For example, it's common for preschoolers to have "calendar time." You can get your preschooler started by playing with and exploring their own calendar at home.

Stewie's Mom: How can parents prepare themselves and their child for the emotional side of starting school?

Experts: It's just as important for the parents to be emotionally ready. We all have our personal memories of how it felt to go to school. The self-aware parent separates his or her childhood from her children's. Focus on empathizing with your child and providing a rock of confidence in them to help them navigate this exciting new experience.

One common way is to ask your children what they are looking forward to and what they are afraid of about starting school. Have these types of sharing conversations several times well before the start of school.

Stewie's Mom: What about the actual moment of bye-bye? That can be scary for the child and the parent.

Experts: Check in with your school to find out what is recommended. And then help your child understand how bye-bye is going to happen. It's important to make this part of the routine. You can say, "I'm going to come in and give you a special school hug and kiss, help you find something fun to do in the classroom, you can show me one thing, and then I go bye-bye." Practice it at home, and if you can, in the actual classroom.

It's important to remember that when your child cries or protests, you naturally feel concerned. Your child can sense you're concerned, which can make them even more upset. Parents must make an effort to focus on their confidence in the child and the teachers.

Stewie's Mom: Why do some children get upset when they are picked up at the end of the school day?

Experts: Some kids happily wave goodbye in the morning, then burst into tears when they are reunited with their parents in the afternoon. Chances are the child held it together all day and now feels safe to have an emotional release. It's okay to believe the teacher who says, "He had a great day. I don't know why he is upset now."

Stewie's Mom: All three of my kids had different reactions to starting school. What can a parent expect?

Experts: Expect some kind of protest from every child—that isn't unusual and shouldn't worry you. If your child protests very strongly, it's especially important for the child to have a set routine.

Some children show their upset by withdrawing and some act out in a way that gets attention. It's important to pay attention to both types of kids, whether they react to transition by going inside themselves or by acting out. If your child's style changes, whether it is more or less interaction with others, that means it's time to check in with your child.

Stewie's Mom: How long should a parent expect to see these protests or transition behaviors before their child gets comfortable with school?

Experts: Each child has a different temperament and different adjustment period. If in the past your child adjusted to a new babysitter in less than a month, but has not adjusted to school after a month, that could be worrisome. Most people feel that two to four weeks is enough time, but up to three months might be needed to get used to a dramatically new environment and routine, depending on the child and the circumstances.

Stewie's Mom: Why do some kids adjust to school and then later change their mind?

Experts: Some children who have adjusted to school may have waves of resistance later in the year. Expect protests and offer your child extra support readjusting to school after any long weekend or vacation. You probably don't want to go back to work, either.

Stewie's Mom: What can a parent do to help a child through these transition behaviors, whether protesting or withdrawing?

Experts: Talk to them without distractions and with plenty of time to let them express themselves. Let them know you see them changing their behavior and that you care why it's happening. Talk about how it's going at school. Ask what they like or don't like. Let them know their feelings, even of upset, are okay. Make sure they know everyone has trouble getting used to something new, and that it will get better. Reading them books like this one is referred to as "bibliotherapy" and is one of the best ways to help your child adjust.

About the Boomsteins

The Boomsteins came about when one of my children was born with an above-average disregard for authority. Needless to say, he had more than a little trouble adjusting to school. He actually walked right out of his preschool during naptime, after he asked the teacher to "get me outta here."

There were many other shenanigans during his transition to the school day, and in an attempt to help him, I wrote little stories. They started out as rhyming stories about talking trains and fantasy places like Shoving Town, but he seemed to prefer more realistic stories about our unique, loud and loving hodgepodge of a family.

I wrote this story in 2009, but then life happened and I shelved it.

In 2013, Karen Young moved in next door to us. She is a fabulous, talented artist, a former art therapist and a mother. We both have butterfly tattoos, wear Vans, and love to laugh as we watch our kids play in our cul-de-sac. One afternoon I asked if she would be interested in doing the illustrations for a children's book I had written, and so began our lovely and wonderful journey of bringing this mostly true story to life. Every page is written and illustrated with much joy and humor. We hope you love it as much as we do.

Thanks for reading this.

Love,
Christine and Karen

For more resources, including a blank What Happens Next picture schedule you can print out and color with your child, and information about upcoming Boomstein titles please check out **NothingButTheTruth.com**

CPSIA information can be obtained at www.ICGtesting.com
Printed in the USA
VOW10s1935270614

BV00012B/394/P